W9-ASW-206

Contents

Will You Be My Friend?

Bears Don't Swim

Picture Stories

WIND	RAIN
SNOW	SUN

The Old Alligator

Go Away, Mr. Wolf!

TELL ME ANOTHER!

Read-Aloud Stories for the Very Young

By *Mathew Price*

Illustrated by *Atsuko Morozumi*

Alfred A. Knopf New York

THIS IS A BORZOI BOOK PUBLISHED BY ALFRED A. KNOPF, INC.

 Published in the United States of America by Alfred A. Knopf, Inc., New York, and simultaneously in Canada by Random House of Canada Limited, Toronto.
Distributed by Random House, Inc., New York.

KNOPF, BORZOI BOOKS, and the colophon are registered trademarks of Random House, Inc.

www.randomhouse.com/kids

Produced by Mathew Price Ltd.

Library of Congress Cataloging-in-Publication Data
Price, Mathew.
Tell me another! : read-aloud stories for the very young / by Mathew Price ;
illustrated by Atsuko Morozumi.
p. cm.
Contents: Will you be my friend? — Bears don't swim — Picture stories —
Wind, rain, snow, sun — The old alligator — Go away, Mr. Wolf!

1. Animals — Juvenile fiction. 2. Children's stories, English.
[1. Animals — Fiction. 2. Short stories.]
I. Morozumi, Atsuko, 1955– ill. II. Title.
PZ7.P93135Te 2000
[E]—dc21
99-28768

ISBN 0-375-80539-7

Manufactured in China

10 9 8 7 6 5 4 3 2 1

First American Edition: March 2000

Will You Be My Friend?

Little chicks usually
have lots of brothers
and sisters, but there
was one little chick
who had none.

And he was lonely.

"I'm lonely," he said to his father, the rooster. "Will you play a game with me?"

"Not just now," said Father. "I have to practice my crowing. See if you can find a friend to play with."

So the little chick went to see the farm dog. "Will you be my friend?" he asked the dog.

"Not now," said the dog. "I'm busy."

"Doing what?" asked the chick.

"Guarding the house," said the dog. "Why don't you ask the cat?"

So the little chick went to see the cat. "I'm all alone in the world, and I need a friend," said the little chick. "Will you be my friend?"

"Not now," said the cat. "I'm busy."

"What are you doing?" asked the chick.

"Hunting," said the cat.

"Hunting what?" said the chick.

"Mice, of course," said the cat. "Go ask the old goat."

The old goat was
munching hay behind
the barn. "Old goat,"
asked the little chick,
"will you be my friend?
Or are you too busy
as well?"

"Busy?" said the old goat.
"Hmmm. Not too busy.
Just let me finish this hay."
And the old goat kept on
munching and munching
and munching.

"Well, who can I play with?" said the little chick.

Just then, a big red fox jumped out of the hedge beside him.

"Play with me," said the fox. And he grabbed the little chick in his mouth and galloped off toward his den.

“COCK-A-DOODLE-DOO!” crowed the rooster. “A fox! A fox! A fox!”

The dog, the cat, the old goat, and all the other farm animals heard the alarm. They stopped what they were doing and ran after the fox.

When the fox saw all the animals chasing after him, he dropped the little chick and ran for his life.

And he never came back.

After that, the little chick found he had lots of friends–and there was always someone to play with.

THE END

Bears Don't Swim

It was a beautiful summer's day. Bear was in his hammock when his friends stopped off to see him on their way to the beach.
"It's a great day for a swim, Bear. Are you coming?" they said.
"No, no," said Bear. "Bears don't swim."

"We've got honey sandwiches," they said.

"Honey sandwiches!" said Bear.

"I'll get my bike," he said.

Bear didn't care where he went, as long as there were honey sandwiches when he got there. So they all set off for the beach.

When they got there, Bear spread his blanket on the top of the sand dunes and settled down to eat the sandwiches.

"I do love honey sandwiches," said Bear.

"But *why* do they go so fast?" And he sighed.

And fell asleep.

His friends were having a wonderful time on the beach below. They never noticed Bear roll over in his sleep . . . and over and over . . .

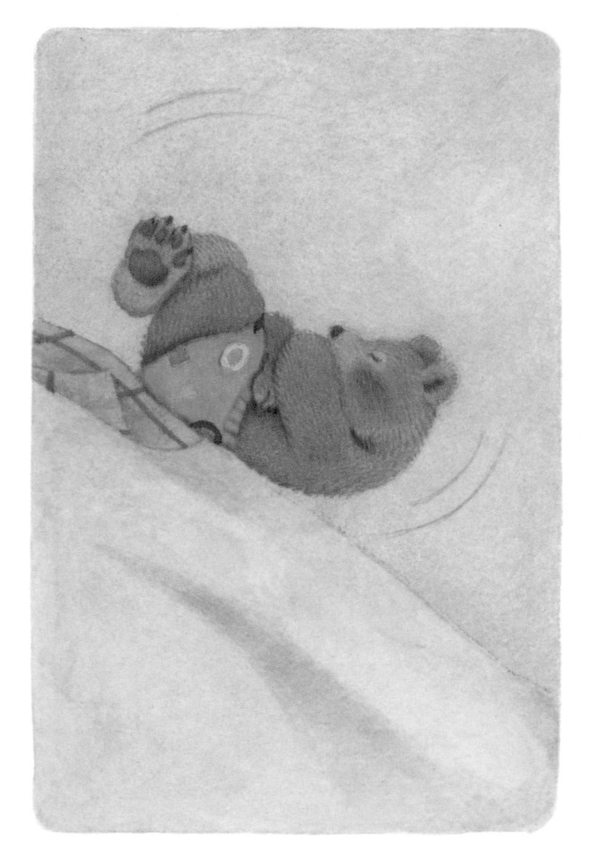

and over . . .

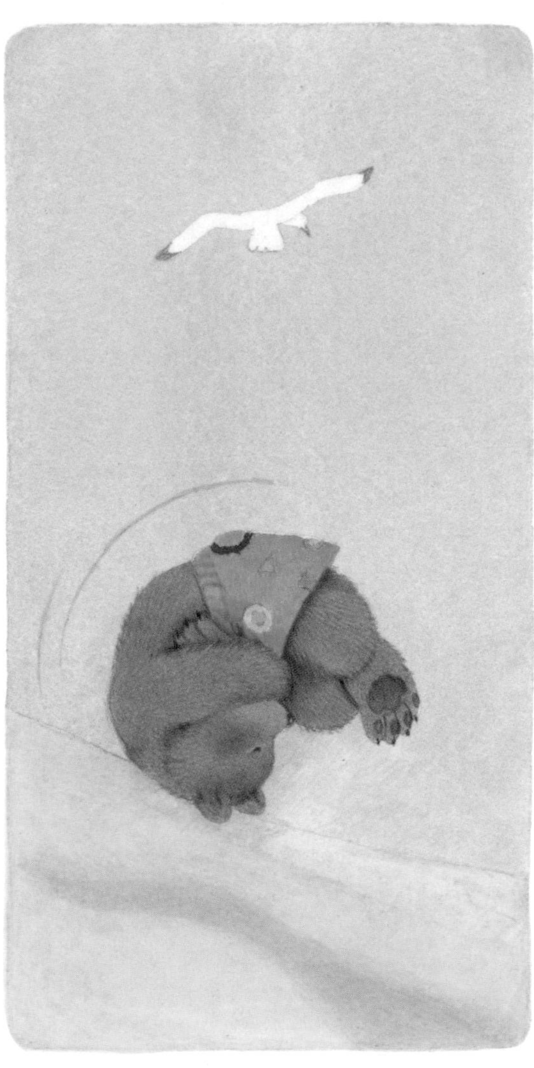

and over . . .

until suddenly . . .

"Help!" he called.

"I can't swim!"

"Bears don't . . ."

"Wait a minute . . ."

"I've changed my mind."

"Bears do swim!"

And swim he did. Bear found out that he loved swimming as much as–well, as much as honey sandwiches.

So he swam

and played

all day long.

He was still swimming long after it was time to go home.

After that, Bear swam as often as he could. When the winter came, he went to the swimming pool and swam there. "Just imagine," he said, "bears *can* swim!"

THE END

Picture Stories

This series of four busy pictures invites you to make up your own stories about all the things that are happening in them.

Wind

Rain

Snow

Sun

THE END

The Old Alligator

Join in the fun by following the instructions for acting out this story.

THREE little ducks were playing in the river,

When along came an alligator, looking for his dinner.

Shade your eyes like the alligator and look out for your dinner.

The old alligator went SNAP! SNAP! SNAP!

Clap your hands 3 times—
Clap, clap, clap.

And TWO little ducks were left.

TWO little ducks were swimming for their lives,

But the old alligator gave a great big smile.

Pull the sides of your mouth wide with your fingers.

The old alligator went SNAP! SNAP! SNAP! *Clap, clap, clap.*

And ONE little duck was left.

ONE little duck was trying to reach the bank, *Make paddling motions with your hands.*

But the old alligator was much too fast.

The old alligator went SNAP! SNAP! SNAP! *Clap, clap, clap.*

And NO little ducks were left.

The old alligator climbed up the bank with
THREE little ducks inside. *Rub your tummy in a circular motion.*

A baby elephant, passing by, stumbled on the alligator, squashing him flat. *Slap your hands flat on your knees.*

Out popped the little ducks, POP! POP! POP! Clap, clap, clap.

And scampered back to Mommy as fast as they could go.

"Oops," said the elephant, "sorry about that."

But that old alligator was FLAT! FLAT! FLAT! *Slap your knees 3 times.*

THE END

Go Away, Mr. Wolf!

Knock!
Knock!
Knock!
Who's that knocking at our
little front door?

"Anyone for ice cream?" said a funny, furry voice.

Knock!
Knock!
Knock!
Who's that knocking at our
little front door?

"Coming for a drive?"
said a charming,
cheery voice.

Knock!
Knock!
Knock!
Who's that knocking at our
little front door?

“It’s a lovely day
for a swim.
Anybody coming
with me?” said a
soft, sly voice.

Knock!
Knock!
Knock!
Who's that knocking at
our little front door?

"Anybody home?"
said a friendly,
familiar voice.